STORY OF A
DOLPHIN

by Katherine Orr

Carolrhoda Books, Inc./Minneapolis

To my parents, with love

First Avenue Editions
An imprint of Lerner Publishing Group
241 First Avenue North
Minneapolis, Minnesota 55401

Website address: www.firstavenueeditions.com

Library of Congress Cataloging-in-Publication Data

Orr, Katherine Shelley.
    Story of a Dolphin / text and illustrations by Katherine Orr.
        p.   cm.
    Summary: Laura's father succeeds in befriending a dolphin who seems to like people, but other people on the island are not so considerate and must be educated in how to respect the dolphin's rights and feelings.
    ISBN: 0–87614–951–4 (pbk.)
    [1. Dolphins—Fiction.] 1. Title.
PZ7.0743St 1993
[E]—dc20
                                                                            92-28656

Manufactured in the United States of America
5 6 7 8 9 10 – JR – 09 08 07 06 05 04

Author's Note

This book is based on the true story of JoJo, a
wild dolphin, who befriended people on the island of
Providenciales in the Caribbean. The conflicts that arose
between JoJo and some humans nearly led to the dolphin's
death. Yet love and insight prevailed. As of this writing,
the misunderstandings that fueled the conflicts have been
virtually resolved. May JoJo and the people of Provo
continue to share a very special friendship that will
show others the way.

It was spring when the dolphin came to our island. We didn't take much notice of him at first because groups of wild dolphins often passed by offshore. They sometimes swam alongside our speeding boat to catch a ride on the cresting bow wave. I loved to watch them play, but they always ignored me and never stayed long.

This dolphin was different. He came alone. He swam along the shore chasing fish in the grassbeds, and he followed my father's dive boat as it carried groups of tourists to dive on the reef.

Almost every day, the dolphin swam to the reef with the dive boat. He carefully watched the tourists dive, but he never got too close to them.

"I think he's lonely," said my father. "He seems curious but also afraid. I want to get to know him, Laura, and perhaps I can become his friend."

Each evening, at sunset, my father went for a swim in the channel. He'd tie his boat to a big white buoy and slide gently into the water. Sometimes the dolphin would come to the buoy and swim nearby.

On weekends and days when I finished my homework early, my father took me swimming with him.

"Don't try to touch the dolphin," my father cautioned. "We'll watch him and he'll watch us, and slowly we'll get to know each other. If he wants to let us touch him, he'll let us know."

The dolphin seemed curious about everything, and mischievous too. He prodded a turtle and played with fish and even sneaked up behind us for some quick tugs at our flippers!

Sometimes the dolphin made clicking noises and whistles. It felt as if the clicks went right through my body.

"He's checking us out with sound waves," my father explained.

Soon the dolphin learned to meet my father for their evening swim. During many months, the two of them slowly became friends. The dolphin allowed my father to touch him, and they played short games of tag. Sometimes the dolphin even took my father's arm in his jaws.

"That's how dolphins play," said my father. "If
he puts his teeth on your arm, Laura, let him
hold it until he lets go. If you yank your arm
away, you could cut yourself by mistake."

The dolphin hadn't touched me yet, but sometimes he swam so close it was hard for me not to reach out and feel his sleek, shining skin.

Then one day the dolphin swam up beneath me and gently touched his dorsal fin along my arm. He circled around and came alongside again with his fin near my hand.

"I think he's offering you a ride," said my father. "When he comes 'round again, just hold on gently and let him pull you." As the dolphin passed by me a third time I held ever so lightly onto his dorsal fin. A moment later I was speeding through the water beside him! The short ride left me breathless and smiling so wide I thought my face would split.

Summer came, and school was out. My friends and I spent our days fishing and climbing sapodilly trees to eat the round fruit that tasted like brown-sugar pears. But swimming was our favorite pastime. This year, swimming was a special treat because the dolphin often joined us. He swam among us like a giant submarine and leaped over our heads as we splashed near shore. He was becoming braver around groups of people, and we really had fun with him.

But sometimes there were problems. Once, we'd all left the water except Annie. The dolphin stayed between her and the beach and would not let Annie come ashore. Annie began to cry, and her big brother ran back to rescue her. As he helped her ashore, the dolphin swam near and gave Annie's brother a smack with his powerful tail. The slap was so hard Annie's brother stumbled and fell. His face turned red and twisted, and as he got up he muttered angry words to himself.

Word spread about the wild dolphin who loved human company, and more tourists than ever visited our island to swim and dive with him. Morning and afternoon, my father's dive boat was full of tourists.

A special trust had grown between the dolphin and my father, but the dolphin was not always so trusting of other humans. And as the number of human playmates increased, the number of troubling incidents grew as well.

One day the dolphin's teeth cut a woman on the arm, and she had to get stitches. Several days later, he smacked a tourist so hard that the man was black and blue for a week. People were growing angry and afraid. Something had to be done, so a public meeting was called to discuss the problem.

The meeting room was hot, and everyone was excited.

"That animal is mean and dangerous," Annie's father exclaimed. "No one is safe while he roams our shores. We have to get rid of him."

"That's right," shouted a fat man sitting up front. "Why, that animal grabbed my hand and swallowed the gold ring right off my finger!"

"And you deserved it, Martin!" called a lady in the back row. "The dolphin grabbed your hand because you were trying to put your finger down his blowhole. He's a joyful spirit who deserves our protection!"

"He's a mystical guide come to teach us wisdom," added someone else.

"Wisdom-shmisdom," growled a man named Ken. "He pushed me into deep water. I could have drowned."

Then my father shoved his way to the front of the room and announced that he had an idea.

"We all seem to have different feelings about the dolphin," he said. "I don't think we can agree about him among ourselves. Why don't we invite a dolphin expert to come and help us. Someone who knows about dolphins could give us advice."

Everyone agreed that it was a fine idea, and soon a dolphin expert arrived on our island. Joan had studied dolphins for many years and knew a great deal about them. She swam with the dolphin and talked to people about their experiences with him.

Finally Joan called a meeting to report her findings.

"I am happy to say that I think there is no need to destroy the dolphin," she announced.

Several people cheered. My father winked at me, and I grinned back. Annie's father grumbled and shook his head.

"These problems between dolphins and humans are caused by lack of understanding, and not because dolphins mean us harm," she continued. "This is a kind-hearted dolphin who needs to learn some things about how to treat people. He tried to keep Annie from coming ashore because he wanted her to stay and play awhile longer. The dolphin pushed Ken into deeper water for the same reason.

"The dolphin may not understand that some people are better swimmers than others," Joan explained. "But dolphins can learn to recognize hand signals and understand what the signals mean. We can teach him how to treat people.

"But the dolphin is not the only one who has something to learn," she continued. "The people who play with him need to learn how to treat dolphins.

"Dolphins don't like hands reaching out and grabbing them, or hands waving near their eyes and ear holes," she said. "The dolphin got upset when Martin tried to put his finger in the blow-hole because that is where dolphins breathe."

"I think you're right!" said a woman in a yellow dress. "It's not right for strangers to touch people in sensitive places. We shouldn't expect it to be all right to treat an animal this way either."

"Exactly," Joan said. "We can learn to behave well toward the dolphin and teach him to behave well toward us."

Joan asked my father to help her set up a training program for people and for the dolphin. She said that the dolphin and my father already understood each other. Their shared trust and respect would help the others to learn.

Soon signs were posted along the beach showing people where not to touch the dolphin. Every Friday night there was a lecture about the dolphin for tourists at the nearby hotel. Joan and my father began teaching the dolphin to understand simple hand signals. The most important signal was a wagging finger that meant, "no, don't do that." My father never gave the dolphin food for behaving well, because he didn't want the dolphin to become a beggar. The dolphin's only reward was my father's attention and company.

Both dolphin and humans began to learn. As the months passed, the number of frightened visitors and bandaged fingers dropped to almost zero, while the dolphin's friendly playmates grew and grew in number. Even Annie's big brother came to love the dolphin and forgave him that slap.

Still, there was one puzzle that remained unsolved. Dolphins, like people, live together in groups of their own kind. Why did this dolphin like to spend so much time with people? Sometimes he was seen with other dolphins. Why didn't he stay with them? Even the dolphin expert had no answer. But one thing was clear: the dolphin loved to be with people. He especially loved my father.

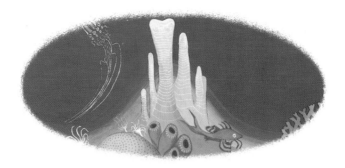

Long hours of time spent together can lead to understanding and real friendship. My father and the dolphin have a friendship like that. On calm moonlit nights, my father goes out to the buoy and calls to his friend by making a noise underwater. Then he slips into the ocean and holds out his hand. The dolphin puts his smooth, hard nose into my father's cupped palm and off they go together, flying beneath the waves. With complete trust, my father lets his friend guide him down through the clear depths and out across the reef. When my father needs to breathe, just a touch of his finger on the dolphin's nose brings them bursting from the sea in a spray of foam and stars.

When I watch them break through the waves together, it is almost like they're dancing. They are dancing a dance of friendship that has helped show others the way.